# Lost Souls
## Becky Mayhew

**photographs**
**Paul G. Vine**

Treehouse Press wishes to thank everyone
who contributed to our funding campaign,
and especially, for their generous support,
David Bjelejac, Kate Griffin, Maggie Hamand,
Colin Herd, Richard Labonté, Bob Merckel,
Sue Oke and Michelle Scorziello.

First published in England
in 2011 by

Treehouse Press
PO Box 65016
London N5 9BD
www.treehousepress.co.uk
hi@treehousepress.co.uk

First edition: September 2011

A catalogue record of this book is available from the British Library

ISBN 978-0-9563775-4-8

design by Raffaele Teo

 printed on treehouse-friendly recycled paper

Thank you to Mum and Dad, for reading every single draft and always telling me I can do it.

And thank you to Joanne Clarkson and Judith Sharpe for unfailing encouragement during A Level English and telling me this is the path I should take.

*For everyone who's ever encouraged me, in any way.*

# Three Stories

# Shelves

Of them all, I suppose Geoffrey was the least offensive. He provided me with a diversion, at least, on selected nights of the week: Tuesdays, primarily – a moderate compensation for the gloom of Mondays – and sometimes Thursdays, as a milepost for the almost complete week. The whole business began when he brought his eighth consecutive John Grisham to the desk, and I made an impassive suggestion that he escape his literary rut and try Austen or a Brontë. It was more for my own vague amusement than a concern for his limited reading habits: I knew this insipid, vole-like little man wouldn't be remotely interested in the feminine meanderings of nineteenth century spinsters, but he took out *Sense and Sensibility*, *Emma* and *Jane Eyre* with boyish eagerness, and exactly four weeks later he returned, looking pale and rather shell-shocked, and lumped the books onto the desk.

He had read them all.

I was impressed. Slightly bemused, but impressed nonetheless: it was a gallant and rather charming attempt to make an impact. Three hefty tomes in four weeks is a meritorious achievement, especially for someone whose literary training lies with Grisham, and, after the last solitary, silent bookworm had disappeared through the doors I granted Geoffrey an hour of my company in the Royal Oak. That was not our first night together *per se* – our first night came a fortnight later when he returned *Wuthering Heights*, and I think the dynamic impression of hot-blooded Heathcliff had gone to his head a little, as he had the audacity to suggest we go back to mine. I conceded, and took him round the corner along the twelve houses to my flat, almost entirely for my own personal interest in what a week of Heathcliff does to a man; as it turned out, less than I had hoped.

His bedroom manner was, although only marginally preferable to the ironing, endearingly mild. Compared to the animalistic approach favoured by Kevin, after which I often had to walk with a duck-like waddle, or the psychotic barraging of Frederick, which left me unable to urinate without pain for nearly three days, Geoffrey's placid lovemaking was rather a relief. His kisses were clumsy and slurping, like I was a dripping ice lolly; his hands were large and dry, and although it often felt like he was caressing me with a pair of gardening gloves, they were not unpleasant, and had the advantage of soothing the plough-lines that Kevin left with his jagged, grubby fingernails. Geoffrey made quiet, meek grunts; Kevin and Frederick had humphed and growled (or roared, in Frederick's case) like crazed bears. The neighbours once intervened, claiming they thought I was being attacked. I apologised for having the television on too loudly and told Kevin to control himself. I suppose one must expect certain coital zeal from a younger man.

As it happened, Kevin's trailing leather coat became entwined round the wheel of the 418 bus one muggy Wednesday morning, and the whole of Epsom High Street was closed off for five hours while they sponged him off the pavement and took statements from traumatised witnesses. It was chronicled in a grammatically-horrendous article in the local paper; I meant to email the journalist responsible and suggest he pay more attention to his Penguin Writer's Manual, but then the Geoffrey business began and Kevin was forgotten. I am reminded of him, occasionally, when I go for my groceries on Monday mornings and I have to walk past the spot where flowers lay wilting and mouldering on the railings by the bus stop. The flowers were replaced frequently for about a month, but, gradually, the browned, perished remains diminished and eventually disappeared altogether.

I saw Frederick recently, outside an insalubrious backstreet pub, one hand up a young redhead's skirt and the other round her throat. I drove past.

Although Kevin's gusto in the bedroom had not corresponded with his listless personality, Frederick's carnal perversions, unfortunately, correlated exactly with his. Geoffrey, conversely, made up for his sexual shortcomings by being fervidly enthusiastic about me. Once, after a typically uninspiring tryst, during which I mentally rearranged my condiment cupboard, he had the deluded gumption to invite me to his monthly night out with the Morden Gentlemen's Operatic Society. I knew exactly what that would entail: a wretched drove of ageing luvvies sipping real ale, fawning over Rodgers, Hammerstein, Gilbert, Sullivan and the rest, and crooning songs from *Showboat* and *Oklahoma!*. I declined, naturally, and Geoffrey was tediously crestfallen.

"But all the wives and partners and girlfriends will be there," he whimpered, fiddling with the tangles of wiry grey hair that sprouted from his breastbone like weeds. "You won't be the only lady... you can talk to the others..."

I firmly reminded him that I wasn't a wife, a partner, or a girlfriend. Geoffrey hung his head mournfully and murmured "I suppose I'd hoped you could be," which was laughable because I'd never given him any reason to make such a supposition.

Unfortunately, I happened to see their production of *Pirates of Penzance*, quite by accident – my pansy of a nephew was in it, playing Third Pirate from the Left, or some such miniscule role – and it was only when Geoffrey bounded onto the stage in a pair of red tights and wielding a plastic sword, his face cartoonish in affable menace, that I realised this was the same society. He couldn't sing. Three lines of a solo sounded like a sea lion caught in a noose. His tights, nevertheless, confirmed what I had suspected: that he dressed to the left.

Despite his ardour for me, his literary inclinations couldn't be turned, and within a couple of months Austen and the Brontës had disappeared and Grisham resurfaced, accompanied at first by a fearful grimace, as though I would slap his wrists and order him back to the shelves, and then with reassured ease, after it became clear I wasn't a starched schoolmistress and actually couldn't give a tinker's cuss about his literary appetite. Our conversations were never scholarly. He prattled about the Operatics, his job (overworked and underpaid at the Home Office), and his father's ailing dog Gerard, and I answered his earnest questions on the technicalities of librarianship and book archiving. I didn't talk about myself, and that seemed to suit him. He was fifty-nine and hopelessly ill-equipped for female company, and I didn't torture him with tales of the esoteric world of women, despite, quite often, having the urge to do just that. Once, during a lull in conversation (in the often excruciating and unnecessary build-up to lovemaking) he said, with an awkward titter,

"So... do you go for Marks and Sparks, or are you a BHS girl?"

I responded by excusing myself and spending a little while in the bathroom to give him time to rethink his approach. When I returned he was nosing through my CD collection and proceeded to pontificate on how *The Rite of Spring* was the determining moment in the neoclassical revolution. When I yawned and looked at my watch (a vulgar warning sign that I only resort to in emergencies), he abruptly stopped, and followed me like a docile puppy to my bedroom.

I tolerated Geoffrey until David borrowed *Lolita*. Young, unshaven, and with inconceivably treacherous black eyes, David was beautiful. He strutted round the shelves like a Roman emperor examining his choice of courtesan, a nonchalant self-importance on his face that at once repelled and bewitched me. His eyes slid like oil over titles, one black eyebrow raised; occasionally he paused to finger a book spine or to bend to a lower shelf, and then he moved on, disappearing and reappearing in and out of the bookcases like a thief. He did not belong in the nauseous, fluorescent light of a library amongst bent heads, yellowing pages and old words: he belonged in shadows, in dark, forbidden recesses whose blackness opened infinite, compelling possibilities. He roused a heat inside me that was agonising after the banality of his predecessor.

Geoffrey was hunched over a Dick Francis when David slid Nabokov across the desk to me, his dark eyes flicking over the buttons of my blouse.

"Do you have your card?" I asked, dry-mouthed.

He slipped his fingers into his wallet, and his shiny card caught the strip light. David Michael Lewis. Account newly opened: no past records.

"Due back in four weeks."

David Michael Lewis took back his card, pulled the book towards him, drifted through the barriers and was gone. Geoffrey bounded up to the desk with his Dick Francis, an inane grin on his face.

Four weeks and three days later, David returned with Nabokov and a thirty pence fine to pay.

"Thirty pence? It's only three days overdue."

"Each day a book is overdue a ten pence fine is incurred."

David stared at me. A flick of ebony hair dangled over his eyes, its point just touching the tips of his eyelashes, convulsing in spasms when he blinked. There was a leaden silence, which I suspected he was deliberately prolonging.

"Every loan is four weeks," I asserted. "Except for oversized books and videos, in which case it's one week."

David glanced at the display of faded video boxes, sleepy 1980s and 90s titles yawning through plastic.

"I don't watch videos."

"Those are the rules," I said, too quickly. "Books are four weeks."

"I wouldn't take out a video," he said, fingering through his pocket. He produced a worn pound coin. "No one watches videos anymore. Videos are obsolete. It's DVDs."

"It's four weeks for books," I said.

David shrugged and slid the coin to me. I slapped my hand onto it, too loudly, to stop it skimming over the edge of the desk, and made Susan look up from her baguette at the next desk. I took out the change from the till and dropped the coins into David's waiting hand.

"I'm not a big reader," he said, looking straight at me, his eyes menacingly still. "I took as long as I needed to read it. A tale of some old pervert's lust for a child is no walk in the park."

His boldness pinched at my stomach and I heard Susan gasp through a mouthful of bread and chicken mayo.

"Nabokov is challenging," I stated, tapping superfluously at my keyboard. "Nevertheless, you can always renew a book if you need extra time."

"Sounds like an exam," David declared, his voice rumbling in the base of his throat, deep and dark. "I thought reading was s'posed to be a hobby, not something with a deadline."

Susan's baguette packet rustled.

"Reading should be enjoyable," I pressed, an unpleasant dampness creeping under my collar. "Nevertheless, there are rules that must be adhered to."

David leaned towards me. His pupils were indistinguishable from his irises: two glassy black marbles.

"Are these your rules?"

"They are those of the library."

"Your library."

"A library operates on the trust that its customers respect those rules as courtesy towards others."

The black marbles gleamed and I watched them roll down to my hand that pathetically, wretchedly, trembled on the computer mouse;

then they stared right at me.

"You need to get out of this place," he whispered, "or you'll get as worn as your books."

He withdrew, and the barriers swung back and forth after him, gradually slipping to a stop.

"What a vile young man," Susan husked pointedly from her chair. "Let's hope he goes somewhere else next time he wants to covet a foul book." She reached across and grasped at *Lolita* with her podgy pink hand. She tutted. "Disgusting. I don't know why we keep books like this. I've been on at Philip for months to have a clear-out. I just don't think it looks very good. I mean, I'm all for important literary achievements etcetera etcetera, but *Lolita*? I just think it's a step too far. You know what it's about, don't you? What it's famous for. It's only famous for being the story of a —"

"Shut up," I said, and went into the office to eat my sandwich.

After David, Geoffrey became as alluring to me as an old sock. In the ensuing weeks I became very familiar with my bedroom ceiling, the one benefit of which was that I realised the extent of the creeping, skeletal cracks in the paintwork, and discovered, after contacting a surveyor, that I had quite a serious case of subsidence, so my time with Geoffrey had a reasonably productive outcome, I suppose. However, our meetings became less regular, and I must gradually have been able to exude an unequivocal air of indifference — perhaps even hostility — as Geoffrey's visits to the library dwindled, and his doleful, injured expression from the Crime shelves eventually vanished with him altogether, and I last saw him when he, rather ashen-faced, returned Ken Follet's *The Pillars of the Earth* — which I expect he'd assumed to be an innocuous book about monks and cathedrals, and it gave me strange pleasure to imagine his trauma at the abundant descriptions of violence and sexual brutality — and I presumed he either joined another library or became an avid television viewer.

I didn't see David Michael Lewis for a while. I began to think I had put him off reading altogether, until he appeared on a murky Friday afternoon while I was restocking the Cookery section with recent returns. His sudden imposing presence in the narrow aisle caused a tightening in my stomach. He ignored me and began peering through the crumpled pages of an old Delia Smith. With any other customer I would have made a routine comment about the reliability of an old leather handbag, or something similar, but, due to the unprecedented moisture inside my blouse, I said nothing, and went about pushing books into their places.

"If I borrow this to cook a meal for my girlfriend tonight, Scout's honour I'll bring it back on Monday," he murmured, not removing his gaze from the Grains and Pulses pages. "I owe her one. She hates champagne and she's on a diet, so chocolate's out. These look reasonably low fat."

He absently flicked the pages in a blurred fan of white and grey. Once again, my mouth was dry.

"Do you know Delia?" he asked dispassionately, never taking his eyes off the wafting pages. "You look like you prefer a low-fat cookbook."

My hand returned a book to its slot.

"Delia's trustworthy," I remarked. "If you're not a cook, she's a good place to start."

He stopped the torrent of pages with his thumb and lifted his head.

"How do you know I'm not a cook?" The thick hush of the library was unbearable. "I could be the next Gordon Ramsey. I could have a Michelin star. You don't know."

A Nigella Lawson throbbed in the hot damp of my palm. For some reason all I could picture was Susan behind the desk, taking great lumpy swallows of carbohydrates.

"Do you cook, then?" I managed.

"Like a king," he replied, cupping the Delia closed with a thick flump. "Which means," he whispered, leaning down closer so I could see the pinprick lines in his lips, "that I don't cook at all." He straightened and tucked the book under his arm. "She does it all. It'll be waiting for me whenever I get home. On the table, steaming and saucy. Just the way I like it."

I thrust Nigella into the nearest slot in a woody clomp that lost itself in the tenebrous realms of the bookcase. Titles and authors throbbed. He was too big, too potent, in these silently pulsing aisles.

"Still, there's always a first time," he drawled, the Delia caught in his grip like a rat in a trap, "so I'd like to take this out, please — if you'd be so kind."

Susan was behind the desk and she could've done it, I knew that, but I weaved out from the mahogany warren and there I was tapping at the till, and there he was across the desk, silently staring.

"Due back in four weeks," I said, but a catch at the back of my throat made me cough. His marble eyes twitched to my mouth.

"Dust," he said simply. "You should get out of this place. Your lungs'll be full of dust. You need fresh air."

I went home and watched television until my eyes hurt, then phoned an old friend who left his son's Maths homework and told his wife he was going for a drink with a colleague.

David Michael Lewis returned the book the following Monday. The ripped, muddied ends of his jeans trailed on the thin carpet.

"Just as I promised," he said quietly, gliding the book across the desk. "When I make a promise I always follow through. I hate to disappoint."

"Did she enjoy it?" I asked, scanning the Delia and slotting it into the returns trolley.

David looked at me blankly and I suddenly had a panicky conviction that he would smirk and drawl, "She always enjoys it," so I hurriedly added, "The meal, I mean."

David waved his hand in the air between us.

"Oh, I never cook. We got a takeaway. Watched a couple of movies, went to bed. All clean, family fun."

Gleams streaked through his dark voice like headlights through rain. I stared at the glowing computer screen, waiting for him to leave; instead, he leaned forward and rested his elbows on the desk, frighteningly close.

"What did you do?"

My stomach knotted.

"I'm sorry?"

"What did you do with your evening? Did you cook a culinary masterpiece or did you slum it and get a takeaway like the rest of us on a Friday night?"

Layers of blankness like empty shelves hung in my head.

"I had dinner with friends," I said, dreadful and gabbled.

"Dinner with friends, eh?" David raised an eyebrow. "Well I never. A socialite. And there was me thinking librarians went home to their cats and their knitting needles."

The sharp sprouting bud of a headache jabbed at my right temple.

"Well — stereotypes are enduring."

"Doubtlessly. So what is it tonight? A bar? A club? Party? Or are you having a night off with a cup of tea and the soaps?"

There were coils of such appalling sarcasm in his voice that, horrendously, a tremor seized my throat and I swallowed, disgustingly loudly; I didn't know where to look, the strip light licked everything in hideous, sickly yellow, and Susan trundled out of the office munching on a cinnamon whirl, her rotund mass swallowing up what little space there was behind the desk. She plonked herself down in her chair and looked disapprovingly at David. She had a shining fleck of icing on her uppermost chin, and her eyes narrowed so sanctimoniously that I wanted to fling the contents of the returns trolley at her stupid head.

"I'm actually having a couple of close friends over for drinks," I said, opening the log book and scanning the pages for nothing. "Just informal — few nibbles, some wine. Nothing fancy."

David Michael Lewis straightened up and thrust his hands into his pockets.

"You *are* busy," he said. "I couldn't keep up with you. Such a hectic, stimulating social life."

His thin lips slid into an unctuous smile, and his left eye flickered in the faintest hint of a wink, then he turned, glided through the barriers, and the doors let in a gust of damp air before thumping shut.

"That nasty young man again," Susan sneered, repugnantly lapping icing off her fingers. "Back to borrow another insanitary book, I suppose."

When I locked up twenty minutes later, David was sitting on the bench by the wheelchair ramp, one heel resting on a knee, a roll-up smouldering between his fingers. In a streetlamp bath of milky orange.

I don't know why it didn't occur to me to lead him round the corner to mine; I don't know whether he followed me or I followed him back to the double doors of the library, where I jangled the keys that hadn't yet made it to my pocket, and slipped through the barriers that slapped our thighs and swung uselessly in the dark; and I don't know who followed whom to the back row of silent, musty wood, where my back ground against the thin horizontal vertebrae, the ranks of books rattled in their shelves, and the mildewed, fusty silence lit up our grunts and pants like creatures in a wood; and where, afterwards, it seemed almost medieval, almost dangerous: dank corridors leading away to black, faraway cells.

I tried to stop breathing; it was vile, embarrassing: the way it grazed the stifled air, the way I couldn't control it. David Michael Lewis leant against the bookcase, one elbow perched on the G–H shelf. His face draped in old darkness.

When he spoke, his voice sank instantly into the gloom.

"I wonder how many times these books have been read."

The shelf groaned slightly as he pushed himself away; his solid, black presence left me, and there was just empty space. Luminous dust drifted in a shaft of street light through the window as the floorboard by my desk creaked under his feet and an abrupt flash of busy air was swallowed shut with the door.

My breath rasped in the stale silence, and tired books looked on from silent shelves.

Ramona

My A Level class is difficult. When they're not texting on their mobile phones, or making mindless jokes (mostly at my expense), or writing notes to each other in margins, they're asking irrelevant questions, or yawning dramatically and gazing out the window. In a class of just seven students, I have never once, in almost two terms, had full attendance; although Ramona Manson, to do her justice, attends every lesson — not that this fact renders her the most able.

Ramona listens well, on the whole, but is prone to daydreaming, and her intellectual input is enthusiastic but often deficient. Nevertheless, at least she makes the effort. It is depressing trying to teach a class of idiots who are far more interested in their social and sexual status than in how Margaret Atwood develops her characters, and nigh on impossible to recover silence when chaos erupts, no matter how visual are my threats of phone calls to parents. It is often, actually, Ramona Manson who orders calm, and it is somehow restored. I don't know why they listen to her and not me: she is not charming, not beautiful, she is not even particularly threatening — she just tells them to shut up and it is done.

This afternoon, a prime example of dire attendance and minimal interest, there are four students: Ramona, Jennifer, Daniel and Grace. Making Atwood engaging for four students who are clearly uninterested (and, in the case of Daniel, almost intolerant) is incredibly disheartening; but then, I am old and unappealing. It must be awful for them to suffer me twice a week. I know what they think of me: I am a tragic old bat with a dated Volkswagen and clip-on earrings. Well, I'm sorry: but we can't afford a new car and I'm not having holes punched through my ears.

They hand in their first drafts of coursework on *The Handmaid's Tale*. Jennifer and Grace's will be repetitive, unstructured and totally obtuse; Daniel's will be a string of incoherent scribbles that supposedly represent "words", but most of which I don't dignify by attempting to locate in the dictionary; and Ramona's will be brimming with superfluous description and half-formed, albeit imaginative, ideas, and she'll be disappointed when I tell her to revise it, as I often do. In the run-up to the last coursework deadline I scheduled extra lessons with her, and spent many hours in stuffy classrooms trying to drum the concept of quality over quantity into her head while caretakers vacuumed round our feet. I had been on the verge of extending the deadline but she got it in at the last minute.

I watch for warning signs during the lesson, but they seem to be quiet today. Probably concocting something. My suspicions are confirmed when I leave the room to retrieve a folder from the staffroom, and find, on returning, that my pen has disappeared. Four perfectly straight faces gaze solemnly at their books. I calmly enquire as to the whereabouts of my pen. There is silence. They are accomplished at this — the Year Sevens and Eights would be hysterical by now, and delightedly informing me I'm losing my memory. There is never any reasoning with them, nothing I can ever do.

I ask Grace, who is nearest, for my pen.

The air is rigid with restrained laughter.

"I haven't got it," she whines pathetically.

It's all so damned perfect for them: I can't search the room for the blasted thing while they sit there and watch me, knowing exactly where it is, I can't go and get another one to come back and find the original on the desk and a room full of smirks. I feel that usual stupid tightening in my throat and my palms grow as clammy as a frightened child's. I don't have another bloody pen. I grip the sides of my chair, and clench my teeth against the need to give in, to beg, to say *please* let me have my pen back.

Ramona Manson finally tuts.

"You can borrow mine, Mrs Linley," she says. She holds out a chewed biro. The strip-light winks in her sepia eyes.

I snatch the pen from her. She rummages in her bag and brings out another equally gnawed biro.

I open my copy of *The Handmaid's Tale* and feel hot moisture swell under my arms. On my left, I hear the guarded snorts of Daniel and Grace. On my right, Ramona Manson's syrupy head is bent, and she studies her book, chewing silently on her pen.

When I get home, I find that Paul has left the front door unlocked again. He was sleeping when I left this morning, after not getting in till gone two. I gathered his late train had been delayed. There is a scrawled note on the kitchen table informing me he has another meeting tonight and probably won't be back for dinner. I heat up a salmon en croute for one from the freezer.

Not locking the front door was never an issue at our last house. It was in a quiet, flowery village, with unlocked front doors all over the place. Here in London it is not quiet. Paul fitted a new burglar alarm when we moved in a year ago: he wanted me to feel safe as he would be away so much. It's a big house, all high ceilings and wooden floors; Paul wanted somewhere we could "entertain". Our friends from the village visited a couple of times in the first few months, then became too busy. Paul's new work colleagues in London don't mix work with pleasure. Most of the staff members at school are younger than me; I don't have much in common with them. There was, early on, David Motley, Head of Music, who took it upon himself to show me round and introduce me to people. I was grateful, but couldn't take to the thick white spittle that gathered on his bottom lip, or the copious dandruff. When a new history teacher arrived — 34, blonde, and apparently very alluring — David Motley no longer ate his banana sandwiches with me. He smiles at me in the corridor now, says "Good morning" apologetically.

After the salmon en croute, I finish the book I've been reading. Ramona Manson had asked me about it when I bumped into her in my local newsagents about a month ago. She'd just started working there and had seen the book reviewed in one of the papers and wanted to know if I'd read it, to give her some indication of whether she should give it a go. I told her I was surprised she should have even the slightest interest in my literary opinion, as her coursework clearly tells me she doesn't spend much time listening to me in lessons. I bought the book. It's not really my cup of tea, but I suppose it's constructive to learn a little of what one's students might enjoy.

I go to bed early. I expect Paul won't be in till late. He works very hard, and long, variable hours.

Paul is still snoring two hours after I get up. I'd heard the front door open and close at half past one, the creak of the seventh stair, the sound of teeth being scrubbed, and smelt thick mint as he dropped into the other side of the bed. When his breathing steadied, I went downstairs and put the latch on the front door.

I am just preparing to leave for the milk when he trudges down the stairs in his weekend clothes: a pair of slacks from the Marks and Spencer's sale in 1998, and a faded maroon shirt from the Marks and Spencer's sale in 1996. His thinning hair flicks up in tufts. I tell him where I am going.

"Ah," he nods, and turns into the kitchen, scratching the back of his head.

I put on my coat.

"Er..." he says. I pause halfway out the door. "I quite fancy a spot of that nice nutty bread from the bakery — and maybe a sticky bun, or something."

I say I'll pick some up.

"Mm..."

He teeters indecisively on the edge of the kitchen. The door latch digs into my palm.

"No, it's all right," he says finally, clearing his throat. "I'll come with you. Yes, I'll do that. We can go together. Why not?"

Before I can say anything, he's shuffling his feet into his slip-ons.

We walk to the high street. Paul tells me about his nightmarish journey last night: trains delayed, incompetent station staff, eight carriages' worth of people crammed into four. He has to go to Norwich, Monday to Wednesday, for an engineering fair. He'll hopefully be back Wednesday night, but if it's too late, he'll most likely get a room at a Travelodge.

When we reach the high street, I tell him to go ahead to the bakery while I get the milk.

"Righteo."

The milk is at the back of the shop. One pint of semi, one pint of full-fat, which is for Paul, but in which I will dabble if I'm feeling up to it. I no longer watch my weight. My body does whatever it wants nowadays, with or without my consent.

Ramona is behind the counter, her maple-blonde hair an untidy torrent over one shoulder. She is chewing absently and flicking through a tabloid. She looks up when I put the milk on the counter.

"I wondered where you were!" she chirps, flapping open a plastic bag. She glances at the time on the till. "Almost seven minutes late this morning – I was beginning to think you'd been kidnapped!"

She is always lively. I have mentioned before that she should think about putting more of this energy into her coursework.

Ramona shoves the milk into the bag.

"Exciting day of marking ahead?" she grins, tapping at the till keys.

Generally, I've found that most pupils have no desire whatsoever to discover what their teachers do at weekends; in fact, I believe they think we fade out of existence on Friday afternoon, to slowly flicker back into the air on Monday morning, like the picture on an old television set. Ramona always asks, though, when I go in for the milk. I tell her yes, I will probably spend most of the day marking.

"Well, have fun," she smiles, handing me the bag, "and I'll see you tomorrow. I'll have a perfect copy of *The Independent on Sunday* ready and waiting!"

I thank her, alert for possible echoes of sarcasm, and leave. I can never tell with Ramona: any disdain she almost certainly has for me isn't as glaringly obvious as it is in others.

I can see Paul through the bakery window, bent down and peering at cakes in the glass cabinet. I wait against the newsagents' wall. A group of young lads trundles round the corner. I hold my bag closer to me: an instinctive reaction, which appears to have developed with age. The boys come to a halt a little way away, lean on their bicycles and light cigarettes, which none of them are old enough to be smoking. The high street is noisy. I watch a woman pushing a pram over the zebra crossing. A sudden shout carries to where I'm standing, and I manage to catch myself before I turn my head.

"Been stood up, Granny?" I hear. Then laughter.

"Need some company while you wait, Gran?"

More laughter, and then the floodgates open to a tirade of similar such yells, all in thrilled, jeering tones, delighted to find a middle-aged woman standing against a wall by herself. I can't walk away now because I am so pathetically obviously waiting for someone that it would clearly be seen as an escape. They yell and snarl, more vulgar each time, stepping out of the group to shout, then slipping back in, congratulating each other on the inventiveness of their insults. People passing glance up, and a couple of men snigger at me; at me, standing alone with my stupid shopping bag held to my stomach, not saying anything while I get publicly trounced by children.

"Your bloke don't like old pussy?"

I glance at the window of the bakery, my cheeks in flames: Paul is there, on the other side of the glass door, his hand frozen on the handle, staring at the group of lads. He doesn't move.

I turn my head away, and focus on the post box across the road. I hate the wretched, quivering bulge in my throat and the smarting behind my eyes. The boys howl a few more insults before getting bored and wheeling their bicycles away, still laughing.

A few moments later, Paul appears beside me carrying a paper bag, through which freckles of sugary grease are seeping. He nods his head towards the departing group.

"Lively bunch, eh?" he chuckles. He clears his throat. "They weren't, er – giving you any trouble, were they?"

I push myself off the wall and walk down the high street. Outside the dry cleaners, Paul asks me again; I say no, they weren't giving me any trouble.

"That's good," Paul says, like a child excused for a wrongdoing.

At lunchtimes, I eat my salad in the English department staffroom. I always eat in here because most of the other English teachers usually go to the canteen for lunch, and I find an hour of peace reasonably rejuvenating. The staffroom is across the hall from Ramona Manson's form room. The form room is typically boisterous at lunchtimes, but Ramona somehow manages to remain separate, and relatively undisturbed, from the furore, which must be by personal choice rather than an enforced decision by her classmates, as she is, by all accounts, a popular member of the form.

She sits at a table in the corner, eating sandwiches from tin foil and reading books. She keeps a pile on the table, and flicks through each book for a few pages, puts it down, and picks up another – a rather erratic method of attempting literariness, but it demonstrates a certain enthusiasm, I suppose, even if it doesn't manifest itself in her coursework. This disparity between her enthusiasm and her attainment has been observed by previous teachers, according to her reports, which I keep at home so I can refer to them with more ease. I tend to consult them in the evenings, when Paul is away.

If I sit at Mary Hampshire's desk to eat my salad or do my marking, I can just about see Ramona, as long as an obnoxious student isn't draped across a desk or dancing to awful music from a mobile phone (when either instance occurs, I intervene, with predictable failure). Twice this lunchtime, two separate groups of friends have traipsed into the form room and hovered round Ramona's desk, trying to get her to go somewhere with them. There is laughter and chattering for a few minutes before the friends give up and leave. Ramona can never be persuaded to leave her books and sandwiches.

I am wishing I had put a little more dressing on my salad, when a skinny girl I don't know hurries into the form room and battles through the throng of sprawling, shrieking students towards Ramona Manson. Ramona looks up from her book, chewing. I can't hear what's being said, but the girl is obviously upset. Ramona looks concerned, stands up, and hurries round the table to sit next to her. There is some talking from the girl, and Ramona nods and listens; the girl starts to cry, her shoulders shuddering rhythmically, and Ramona puts her arms round the girl and hugs her. I can see her squeeze the girl tightly; then she draws away, looks at the girl and says something. I can't hear what it is, I can't hear over the racket in the form room, not even if I stop crunching on lettuce, but Ramona says something to the girl, and the girl nods, and Ramona rubs her shoulder and says something else, and the girl laughs. Then, after a minute, the girl gets up, waves cheerfully to Ramona, and wanders out. Ramona, nothing discernable on her face, moves back to her chair, picks up a book, and takes a bite of her sandwich.

Precisely on the dot of 1.45pm, the bell in the corridor screams its alarm. I wait at least three minutes to avoid the thundering mass of bodies that storms the corridors – I can hear the shouts and stamps on the other side of the staffroom door, which I have closed, and there is an almighty slam against it, then an enraged yell and threat of retribution, followed by, presumably, a pursuit through the throng to end in physical blows in a faraway classroom. When the rumble of the stampede dies down, and only the unpunctual and the uncaring are left outside, I rinse my salad tub and prepare myself.

I pick up my folders – Year 10, *Lord of the Flies*, hideous – and venture into the corridor.

Classrooms are filled with unruly animals, fronted by teachers who attempt to gain peace; some of whom, like Richard Mack and Joyce Winterman, succeed immediately and with no ounce of trouble, while others, such as Karen Morris and Graham Deane, are less victorious, resorting to panicked begging or distraught surrender (either method delights the class).

I walk the length of the corridor, and, at the top of the stairs, there is a group of four Year 11 boys. I know two — Jack Merchant and Alex Fisher — as I have taught them before. They are 16 years old, untouchable and impossibly arrogant, afraid of nothing and no one — and, like the rest, they have the same dogged scorn for me as they have for any other authoritative figure.

They are loitering in the corridor, scuffing their shoes, each with his tie done up in a different, equally ridiculous fashion; they look as though they have been festering in a malodorous bedroom for God knows how long, slashing each other to pieces on computer screens or raving about pitiful sexual conquests. Alex Fisher spies me and smirks disgustingly, then looks me up and down, and his look of delighted derision whips up a fury inside me, and I know it would be safer to ignore them and walk on, but the little brats are so confident, so indestructible, that I am suddenly and almost uncontrollably compelled to challenge them.

"What are you doing?" I ask, looking directly at one of the ones I don't know, as he appears the least menacing.

"On our way to class, Miss," the boy replies, in faux-innocence.

Jack Merchant nudges him towards me, and as our faces come perilously close, I am swathed in the thick, sour stench of rancid nicotine.

"You've been smoking," I say, too quickly, too eager to grab a weapon.

"Nah, haven't, Miss," he replies.

"I can smell it. You've all been smoking."

"We haven't, Miss," Jack Merchant drawls.

They loom in, forming a preying circle. They are taller than me apart from the first speaker, and if I continue to goad him it will be painfully obvious that I am threatened by the others; so I turn to Alex Fisher.

"You've been smoking. That is against school rules, as well you know. You will all go down to the deputy's office this instant."

Alex Fisher looks at me, cruel eyes unwavering. The others snigger in anticipation of a bloodcurdling response. He simply shrugs his shoulders.

"Nah."

The others erupt — they would've laughed whatever he had said.

"What do you mean, 'Nah'?"

"Nah."

"Do you mean you're refusing to go?"

He shrugs again.

"Or do you mean you haven't been smoking?"

"Nah."

"So you admit you have been smoking?"

"Nah."

The others hop up and down, whipping their fingers together, taking great, gleeful, stupid gasps through grinning teeth as they marvel at their leader. Alex Fisher merely stands, chewing, looking down at me.

"Alex Fisher, you will go downstairs this instant," I say, nausea rising as I hear the anguish in my voice. My folders are hot against my stomach, which is suddenly huge, and that's that damned full-fat milk.

Alex Fisher leans towards me, having to stoop to come down to my level. The acerbic stench of cigarettes plasters my face, and he full knows it.

"I ain't been smoking," he says slowly, "and I ain't goin' downstairs. I'll be late for class, innit."

"You don't care a bloody jot about being late for class!" I cry, my voice straining like a child in the midst of an inconceivable injustice.

The boys draw air through their teeth and I know instantly that I have lost; there is no going back now.

"You swore, Miss," Jack Merchant gloats. "We're not allowed to swear — in't that what you tell us? You're supposed to be settin' an example. What if I told my mum our teacher swore at us? She wouldn't be happy."

"Neither would mine," pipes up the hitherto silent one. That is his contribution, and he will be proud of it for the rest of the day.

"My dad hates swearing," says Alex Fisher. "He whacks me when I swear. He'd be well angry if he found out a teacher swore at me. *Fucking* angry."

The others are beside themselves. They claw at the walls, slap each other's arms, double up in frenzied mania. Alex Fisher stands before me, in his eyes a satisfied, almost simmering ecstasy at this victory in front of his mates. I shrink against the lockers, my folders to my sagging stomach, floundering. They will have me now: I have lost spectacularly, and they will stay to devour their prey like vultures in a desert.

"Oi," comes a voice through the corridor.

The boys turn. Ramona Manson ambles down the corridor, her bag slung over her shoulder. She looks as though she could be whistling a tune on a Sunday stroll.

"What you lot doing? Shouldn't you be in class?" she says, looking at them apathetically. She doesn't see me, cowering against the lockers. I could slip away now, while they're looking at her — anything to avoid being the teacher who trembled like a frightened child, ganged up on by a bunch of boys thirty years younger. But there's no way they would let me slip away: not a chance.

"Urgh, you stink," Ramona says, screwing up her nose and waving a hand in front of her face. "How many fags you had?"

"Not as many as you," Jack Merchant murmurs and the others chortle. Ramona slaps him on the arm.

"Shut up, dick head. I've given up. And if I tell my sister you've been smoking you know she'll chuck you. She hates fags."

She walks right through the middle of them and sees me.

"Oh, hi, Miss."

And that's it.

Alex Fisher nudges her shoulder.

"We were just having a chat with Mrs Linley about swearing," he says.

Ramona looks at him blankly.

"Great," she says, shrugging her shoulders. "But piss off, go to class. You're making me late."

Frustration slips onto Alex Fisher's face — I wonder if he will pursue it — but his cohorts are already scuffing their way up the corridor, so quickly uninterested. Alex Fisher steps back a little, his eyes lingering on me, passing a silent promise of reprisal, then turns and struts after his mates, into a torrent of back-slaps and congratulations, and they disappear into a classroom.

"Kids," Ramona says, staring up the hall and shaking her head. "I was never like that in Year 11!"

She looks at me.

"Are you all right, Mrs Linley?" she asks, frowning. "You look a bit flushed."

"Of course I'm fine," I snap. She is just a little taller than me. "Get off to class, you're late."

Ramona withdraws.

"Yeah, sorry," she breezes; then adds, between half-closed lips, "But it's only General Studies, and we all know that's not a proper lesson!" And she turns and strolls to the stairwell; when her bobbing head disappears below the railings, the corridor is empty.

That night Paul doesn't call as he'd said he would. After tossing and turning, I finally give in and call him, only to be greeted by the automated woman that tells me my husband's phone is switched off. He could have checked in to a hotel, as he said he might. The night drags on, my sleep broken by sudden moments of alertness in which I am totally aware of myself lying upstairs in a big, dark house with humming appliances and ticking clocks and the empty space beside me. At six I call again, then at half past and at seven and when he finally answers at quarter to eight my head is pounding and, as expected, work had gone on too late, he'd missed the last train and had checked in to a Travelodge. I stare at his overnight bag on the wicker chair in the corner of our bedroom as he tells me he will be home tonight.

I drive recklessly to work and rush into my first class several minutes after the bell. Brash conversation continues regardless of my presence, and a sly look from Jennifer tells me they will carry on whether I like it or not. A quick head count: Ramona is missing. She is occasionally late, like most of them.

I slap my folders down on the table and it startles them – a rare gesture of assertiveness they weren't expecting – and my demand that they open their books falls into the sulky silence.

"Anyone know where Ramona is?" I ask.

Corrina shrugs dumbly and the others simply ignore me. Grace is texting on her mobile phone under the table – she thinks I'm stupid, thinks I can't see the muscles flex in her bare arm, and the concentration etched on her face as she peers down into her lap – and I hold out my palm to her.

"Give it to me," I say.

Grace looks up at me with indignant surprise.

"What?" she says.

"Your phone, give it to me."

"I haven't got my phone."

A snigger from Daniel.

"And you," I say, turning on him, "tell us what's so funny. Go on, tell us."

Daniel immediately flicks his eyes to his comrades. They all look at each other, eyebrows raised. I can almost see the messages darting between them across the table, the damned secret language of teenagers that adults can't decipher and can never learn. I glance at the door. The corridor beyond it is deserted. Ramona is almost fifteen minutes late.

I turn back to Grace.

"Give me your phone," I repeat.

"Miss, I haven't got my phone," she protests, and holds up her empty hands. "I left it at home."

"Your dog ate it," mutters Jennifer, and there are snorts from the others.

"I don't think you realise how ri*dic*ulous you are," I snarl, my fist thumping the table in an involuntary spasm.

Real, sudden astonishment leaks into their hard eyes. My chest flutters. I hold my hand out to Grace.

"Give. Me. Your. Phone."

A moment's pause, in which she briefly considers fighting back, then she gives in, bored. She reaches into her lap and drops her phone into my waiting palm. I put it on the desk next to me. The flutter in my chest grows to a swelling. I have triumphed.

"Think you must be on your period, Miss."

Simply a mumble, almost inaudible; a moment when it seems impossible that words had been made from the low grumbling noise, and a conviction that I have misheard; then, as the glee on the faces before me blossoms and flowers, the echoes of the words seem to scream round the table and I know, I know that I heard exactly what I was meant to hear.

"Get out," I say. I can't say anything else. "Just get out. Spend the lesson time reading Atwood, or do what you like. Just get out."

When they stare dumbly at me, I shout, pathetically, hearing my voice begging them to leave me alone, and they scrape back their chairs and trundle out.

"Where is Ramona?" I call weakly to Corrina, the last one out.

"Dunno," she shrugs. "Think she might be sick."

The door clicks shut, not before I hear the eruption of giggles in the corridor.

I fumble in my bag for my mobile phone. I find Ramona's mobile number, which I'd entered as a precaution for instances such as this, and hold the phone to my ear. After a pause, it begins to ring. It rings five times before someone picks up.

"Hello?"

She sounds croaky, half asleep. I put my other hand to the phone and press it against my ear. My mouth is suddenly dry, and when I ask her why she isn't here my tongue sticks to the roof of my mouth and makes a horrible sucking sound. Ramona doesn't answer straightaway, and I realise I didn't say who I am.

"Oh – hi, Mrs Linley. I'm really sorry, I'm not feeling very well today. Got a bit of a bug, I think."

I ask her why she didn't ring.

"I rang the school office." She pauses, and her breath rattles very slightly through the receiver. "Maybe they forgot to tell you. I'm really sorry."

The phone burns my ear. I ask if she'll be in tomorrow.

"Oh, yeah, I expect so. It'll have cleared by then."

"Make sure," I hear myself say. "Make sure you're in tomorrow."

A slight pause, then, "Yeah. Hopefully."

She says goodbye, and the line goes dead. I take the phone from my ear, and it sucks slightly at my cheek. Its plastic cover is smudged with moisture.

I cancel the rest of the day's classes and go home with a migraine. Paul is in the lounge, eating banana on toast in his Y-Fronts. He looks like a startled deer.

"Oh, er –" he says, but I am upstairs before I can hear the rest. His work clothes are slung over the back of the chair in the bedroom. I take them down to be washed, but have to go at his shirt with the stain-remover first because lipstick is so bloody hard to get out.

# Roses

There he is, inside a flaming scarlet halo. Head bent, eyes down. Brown hair dangling over his brow. Blinking once, twice — again. A corner of his bottom lip tucked between his teeth. Every now and then he puts a hand to his cheek, rubs it absently, looks up and about him, his face flushed in the flames. He crosses and uncrosses his legs, slicing them together like rose cutters. People hurry past him — grey, blank-faced people, not seeing the boy swathed in red smoke — but that is the way it is. That is the way it always is: he is there for her. No one else can have him. As long as she is there and he is there, he belongs to her.

Elizabeth draws back from the roses. A long, dull score throbs in her palm where the corner of the display table has furrowed into it. She tweaks at the rose stems and the boy disappears behind their pouting velvet lips.

Their painted faces gaze at her from all around the shop, nodding gently. During the day, they recline like elegant women, silently swooning with willowy arms over faces, heads tilted coyly — but they talk about her when she shuts them up at night, in shrill, giggling voices that brim in the darkness like hungry bees. They talk about her, and about him: how he comes to her, how he always sits in the same place at the same time, just so she can see him. They talk about how perfect it is, and how what they share together is so beautiful. But by day they nod silently at her, watching.

They look at her from under teasing brows.

"Now, now," she mutters to no one in particular, but frowns at the bucket of yellow freesia on the window sill: she knows they are all listening. "How you do gossip!"

She wipes her hands down her blouse. A double-decker bus snarls past, rasping black smoke, and makes the cluster of bamboo shiver in its vase by the door.

"Dirty great thing," she tuts, and strokes the bamboo shoots softly with the flat of her palm. "There now, he's gone. Not to worry."

She takes the clippers to an unruly spray of fern.

An elderly woman hobbles in for a gift for a sick friend. Elizabeth gives her a handful of merry daisies, and the woman thanks her with extraordinary relief, saying that it's *exactly* what her friend needs to "cheer her up." Elizabeth smiles and nods and makes sympathetic sounds, marvelling at this woman's conviction that a fistful of daisies can heal the sick, and helps her down the step. Perhaps she'll be able to sell some of the lilies she over-ordered.

A doddering old man limps in at ten to five and speaks tremblingly and at length about nurturing techniques, while Elizabeth tries to nod politely and usher him out of the shop before he can decide to buy something and waste more of her precious time with a fumbling transaction, but he points at the inky orange tulips with a shrivelled finger and gabbles something about their being his wife's favourites. Elizabeth grabs a few, clumping together their weak green arms, rolls them up — no time for elaborate twists of cellophane, his wife will have to make do with brown paper — and takes his quivering ten pound note from his outstretched hand, which is five pounds less than what they cost, but no matter; steers him through the door as he tells her his wife will be "utterly thrilled," and when he is back on the street and the door is locked she scrambles to peep through the huddle of blushing pink delphiniums, fearing her boy has gone — but there he is. She shakes her head: silly girl, she should have known he wouldn't leave without her.

Her boy looks at his watch, rolls up his magazine, and stands up and stretches. The waitress, that ugly little piglet with stout legs and clipping trotters, toddles out and picks up his empty cup. She says something and smiles inanely, her head scrunching pink neck-flesh into thick rubber bands. He smiles and nods, clearly humouring the foul little piglet; he holds up a hand halfway in a polite wave, and walks away. The piglet watches after him for a few seconds before trotting back through the door.

"That's right," she murmurs, the daisies' soft white fingertips brushing her cheek as she leans forward to watch him go. "He knows

I'm here, he knows I won't let little piggies get him. He waited for me so I could look out for him."

He swims away through a watercolour pool of pink and white.

And sinks into the swirling flushes.

The sunflowers are being cheeky; she can tell the moment she walks in. They stand shoulder to shoulder, staring brazenly at her.

"What are you up to?" Elizabeth says, heaving the metal buckets into their places. "Looking at me like that. Have you been gossiping about me again? You should talk to me directly, not sit there whispering and then pretend you didn't say anything. And don't look so bumptious. Yes, you look very full of yourself this morning."

The white roses gasp, their childish mouths pink with a lollypop hue.

"Don't look so surprised," she says, wagging her finger at them. "Those sunflowers need telling sometimes."

When everyone is in their places, Elizabeth stands in the little square of tiled space and watches the clock on the wall. The snapdragons forever stretch their pining hands to it, but can never quite reach. The minute-hand edges up cautiously.

The minute-hand touches the ten; the hour-hand heaves itself up to the nine.

Sure enough, he emerges into the pallid haze, his bag over his shoulder, his magazine curled up under his arm like a beloved pet. He disappears into the blackness of the coffee shop. He never stays long for her in the mornings, he doesn't have time: he buys a coffee, stops to take a sip just outside the door, discards the lid in the litter bin by the lamppost, and strolls off. It doesn't matter though, Elizabeth understands: he is busy – and anyway, he always comes back to her later.

She doesn't remember when he first started coming to her. In her solitary hours amongst these faces, she had little else to do but look out at the world beyond her window: oblivious strangers hurrying past her, astonishing her at how few she recognised from years of staring out through the same pane of glass. Then she had started recognising him: the boy who appeared across the road. At first she couldn't believe he came back so frequently – no one else did – but he kept on coming, the same times every day. It had taken her a while to realise he must be there for her. He chose the space right in front of her, to be near to her, to feel as comforted by her as she does by him in a world of cold strangers. I am here, he says. I am real.

She waits at the window, nestled in the undergrowth. She taps an index finger on her knee. The lilies hold out their green hands in bewilderment.

"Don't worry, don't worry," she whispers. "He'll be out in a minute. You'll see."

A harsh rap rattles the door. Elizabeth jumps, and the lilies lick at her face.

"Lord, what the devil...?" she growls, scrambling out in rustles and soft shrieks of silver buckets.

An old gentleman peers through the glass with wrinkled hands cupped around his face. Elizabeth shoos her hand at him and shakes her head wildly.

"Not open yet!" she hisses.

The gentleman smiles at her, his face wrinkling like old yellowed paper, and nods.

"Hello?" he shouts through the glass. "Are you open?"

"Not open! Go away, we're not open yet!"

"I need some of the beautiful sunflowers you've got in there." His mouth splatters a dirty grey fog on the glass. "Can I come in?"

A punching in her chest, she fumbles the key into the lock and opens the door a fraction. The old man's creviced face smiles at her through the crack.

"I'd like some of those wonderful sunflowers you have," he rasps. "My granddaughter's just had a baby, you see — my first great-grandchild! Such a pretty little thing! Sunflowers will be perfect —"

"We're not open yet," Elizabeth gasps, the punching in her chest sending shocks through her veins and tightening her throat. "You'll have to come back later. Goodbye."

"But I just wanted the sunflowers —"

"Good*bye*."

Elizabeth slams the door shut and the glass clatters in its frame. She clambers back into her jungle, the daisies bumping against the peacock feathers, and pulls apart the lilies. The petals flutter under her breath like whirring tongues. The coffee shop doorway is black. She can just make out the glint of the brass counter inside.

She waits, breathing slowly and steadily. The shop doorway yawns darkly. There must be a queue; or he's put his wallet in his bag instead of his trouser pocket and he's had to search for it; perhaps they haven't got what he wants and he has to decide on something else. She waits. An elderly couple heave themselves up the coffee shop step as though climbing a stupid mountain. A woman holding the hand of a repulsive screaming child comes out. Then there is nothing but blackness and that glint.

He's gone. She has missed him.

Elizabeth pushes the lilies away from her face. She tastes sudden bitterness on her lip: it is some of the orange venom from the lilies' spiked tongues. She rubs her mouth raw with her sleeve. She stands in the middle of the shop, her heart stamping. The sunflowers beam at her smugly. This was what they'd planned. They did it on purpose, just so she would miss him. It was all a nasty trick.

"You evil little devils," she snarls, raises her arm high, and slaps at their heads. The sunflowers throw their heads back in swishes and cracks, before swinging round to stare at her, unabashed.

"Little *devils*."

She slaps them again, then again. They whip from side to side, bleeding yellow. She slaps them until they can't look at her so brazenly, but bow their heads to stare numbly at the floor, necks broken, dripping brown blood and finally repentant.

"That'll teach you," she whispers. "That'll teach you."

The clock on the wall is sluggishly pulling itself up to five o'clock. She'd seen her boy at lunchtime, in his usual place with his usual drink, and today he'd had a sandwich, as well. He'd eaten it in the waxen lily fog and read his magazine; the piglet-waitress had trotted out and made a stupid joke, and he'd pretended to laugh, just to humour her inanity. In his beautiful embarrassment whereupon he looked around at anything apart from the stupid waitress, he looked straight at Elizabeth; for support, clearly, to know that she was there. She saw him — she was there. The little piggy watched him walk away and called out something to someone in the shop, and then laughed in a revolting, self-satisfied way, thinking that he bears some kind of regard for her.

"As if he would," Elizabeth had muttered, and repositioned the lilies and the peacock feathers so that the coffee shop was concealed behind her faithful little soldiers.

A man and a woman peer in at the window, point at her flowers behind the glass. Say something to each other. Move away without giving Elizabeth a glance. A young woman comes in for a mixed bouquet for her recently engaged friend. Pale pink germinis, snow-white chrysanthemums, sunny carnations.

"Perfect!" she gushes, burying her face in their heads. "They are just *perfect!*"

She shoves money at Elizabeth and bustles out, thoroughly delighted at the wonderful choice she has made. Another, older woman comes for a handful of turquoise gerberas simply to "brighten up the mantelpiece." A scrunch of cellophane, a ripping of sellotape, and she's overjoyed. It's the same, always the same, day after day: these people come in and take her flowers to make their lives more beautiful. And they are so predictable: lilies to say goodbye to dead loved ones; roses to proclaim a sudden rush of love or to whisper a fervent apology; freesias to say a cheery hello or a welcome back; daffodils to simply have on the kitchen table, a pathetic bright bloom of yellow at a family dinner smiles, "We are secure; we are fine." Once in a blue moon a face she recognises comes in, but there is no acknowledgement from either side. There is no point. A business transaction takes place, perfunctory and boring. She is here to serve them, and that is that. Only her boy appreciates her — only he comes to see her every day, over there where she can see him. He is the only one she cares about. Sometimes she can feel him, in the long stretches when she is alone with her flowers; she can feel a presence, a warmth about her, as though he is sitting right there beside her, breathing her perfumed air. Their worlds beautifully interlaced like the coiling infinity of an open rose.

A young girl comes in to collect a pre-ordered birthday bouquet for her mother — sugary pink chrysanthemums, sickly peach gerberas. She drops a crisp twenty-pound note into Elizabeth's palm, bids an obligatory thank you, and dislodges the neat stack of message cards on the counter as she hurries out.

The fern waves her off.

"Don't do that!" Elizabeth snaps. "Don't encourage them."

The fern defiantly waves a little more, then comes to a sulky stop.

"That's better."

Elizabeth takes the big silver key from the shelf. She unwedges the door from its tired halt, rattles the key into the rusty lock and a pair of shoes and legs clatter into the closing door, a hand slapping against the glass.

"Shit, mind out, sorry!"

The shoes and legs speak, and coffee-sour breath blasts onto the top of her head. She looks up, steps back, and he stands there, one foot wedged in the door, one red-knuckled hand closed round the edge.

"Can I just get something really quick?"

The lilies lick their lips gleefully. The bamboo whispers. The sunflowers smile through their bruises, heads drooped to the floor.

"It's for my girlfriend, it's her birthday today and I haven't got her anything. She'll kill me. Can I get something for a tenner?"

Elizabeth stands back and he comes in. He stands in her little space, staring dumbly at the silver pots of sprouting colour. They stand innocently now, not revealing anything; holding up their heads for inspection, gazing blankly and serenely like window models. He points at the roses.

"How much are they?"

Her head is as empty as the glass.

"Two pounds each," she whispers.

He drops his arm. Stubby fingers hang from his overlong jacket. The magazine stays caught in his armpit. He stands in her shop, staring at her flowers. A fingerprint on a painting.

"Oh, I dunno. Every bloke gives roses, don't they? Bit boring. What are those?"

"Lilies."

"They're all right, aren't they?"

"People tend to use them at funerals."

"Oh. She probably won't know that, though. She's not really into flowers."

"Then why are you buying her flowers?"

"Well... dunno what else to get her."

The lights slop on his forehead, white and oily.

"Oh, sod it, I'll just have five roses. Red."

"Five red roses?"

"Yeah."

Five red roses. Elizabeth sees her ashen fingers pull out five roses by their skinny necks, and watches as they set them down on the paper. The roses lie with their heads upturned, staring, mouths open, stick-thin limbs intertwined and limp. She feels him standing behind her; hears him pull her air down into his lungs.

"I never even saw this place before, only noticed it just now."

Elizabeth wraps the roses; like closing dead eyes.

"Bit stupid, 'cause I sit out there every day. How stupid's that?"

Sellotape licks the paper. Elizabeth hands him the sharp bundle. Twisted limbs. Bloody faces.

"I've always been here," she says, looking at him. "I've seen you out there."

He stares at her. A glistening, bulbous boil strains on his cheek. A small brown cluster of dried coffee nestles in the corner of his mouth.

"Yeah?" He glances at the silent flowers by the window, and his mouth slides into a grin. "Ah, yeah, bet you hide behind there and spy on people, don't ya?"

Someone shouts outside.

"I don't," she says quietly. "I see what I happen to see. That is all."

He nods.

"Tenner, was it?"

"Ten pounds."

He rummages a hand in his pocket, pulling out an ancient crisp packet and clumps of grimy paper.

"Christ's sake —"

His magazine slips from under his arm and splatters onto the tiles. A woman, sleek limbs splayed like lily petals, gazes up at Elizabeth, lips slightly apart, eyes dark, fingers like fans on velvet skin.

"Woops!" he grins, bending down to pick it up. "Mustn't break my favourite girl!"

Elizabeth watches the woman disappear in glossy leaves.

"Here it is," he says, and holds out a ten pound note. "Knew I had it, didn't I?"

Elizabeth takes it between a thumb and forefinger. It hangs like a dead leaf.

"Hopefully these'll score me some points with the missus!" he chirps, waving the roses at her. "Cheers for that. See ya later!"

And he drops out of her shop like a stone through a grate.

She stands alone in her quiet, empty space holding the note in her hand. The door creaks as a wind blows in. Flowers whisper and bend their heads to each other, willowy green hands over smirking red mouths. The bamboo chuckles raspingly under its breath. The lilies poke out their tongues; the sunflowers nod on their aching necks, shoulders shaking with weary laughter; the remaining roses purse their lips and twizzle their shoulders like sneering children. They all stand in their gangs, laughing.

Elizabeth steps towards them.

Her arm smacks through the fragile necks of the freesia, spluttering yellow flecks.

The lilies throw back their heads as their necks crack under her hand, spitting orange blood.

The snapdragons lurch backwards from their perch, slamming into the fuchsia, mangled and broken limbs tumbling onto the tiles.

The sunflowers flash in her face as the back of her hand smacks their weak bodies, and they spin from their silver bucket and plummet head first to splatter onto the floor, heads at broken angles. Flowers, petals, leaves and limbs are tossed and flung, exploding like paint.

When she stops, everything is quiet. Flowers dangle from pots, slump against weak bodies; arms wide and bent, dead faces crushed in pools of mottled blood. She stands amidst her silent, shattered rainbow. The air is thick with weeping scent.

She opens her fist and his ten-pound note lies scrunched and dirty in her palm. She tosses it, feels its papery touch leave her fingertips, then watches it disappear into the broken colour.

Becky Mayhew writes short stories, plays and humorous articles. She graduated in English Literature and Creative Writing from the University of East Anglia in 2006. Her ideas and inspiration are accumulated through being at some point a barmaid, teaching assistant for disengaged students, office administrator, and keen eavesdropper, as well as an avid reader. *Lost Souls* is her first published work of fiction.

Paul G. Vine lives and works in Scotland. He is currently a buyer for an Edinburgh-based cooperative.